For Louis
~ C W

For Nina, my god-daughter
~ A E

This edition published by Scholastic Inc., 557 Broadway; New York, NY 10012,
by arrangement with Little Tiger Press.
SCHOLASTIC and associated logos are trademarks and/or
registered trademarks of Scholastic Inc.
Distributed by Scholastic Canada Ltd; Markham, Ontario

First published in the United States by Good Books, Intercourse, PA 17534, 2009

Library of Congress Cataloging-in-Publication Data is available for this title.

Original edition published in English by Little Tiger Press,
an imprint of Magi Publications, London, England, 2009.

Text copyright © Catherine Walters 2009
Illustrations copyright © Alison Edgson 2009

ISBN-10: 1-84895-016-0
ISBN-13: 978-1-84895-016-0

Printed in China

2 4 6 8 10 9 7 5 3 1

The Magical Snowman

Catherine Walters

Illustrated by Alison Edgson

It was a clear, sparkling winter's day. Little Rabbit had been busy all morning, piling snow to make a snowman.

"Good work, Little Rabbit," said Daddy. "Could you finish it later, though? I need you to find some berries for our breakfast."

"Snowman will be sad if I leave him now," Little Rabbit said.

"He'll be fine," said Daddy gently. "He's just a snowman. He isn't real."

"He *is* real!" said Little Rabbit. But Little Rabbit went off to do as Daddy told him.

Daddy smiled as he gave
Little Rabbit a kiss. "Don't
go too far," he said.

"I won't!" said Little Rabbit.

"Mmm, one for the basket and one for me," he sang as he skipped down the lane. Soon his paws were sticky with purple juice.

Little Rabbit was having
so much fun . . .

he hardly noticed the snow
beginning to fall.

A robin flitted ahead of
him and he followed it . . .

dancing through the drifting
snowflakes and bare trees.

Then the robin flew away. Little Rabbit stopped and looked around. He wasn't sure which way he had come. The swirling snow made everything look different.

"What will I do?" he cried. "How will I get home?"

As if in answer, a soft light sparkled through the trees. Smiling through the falling snow was his very own Snowman!

"I *knew* you were real!" said Little Rabbit.
"But, Snowman, I feel so alone."
  "Not all alone," smiled Snowman.
"I was there too, little friend. I am always
  there for you."

Snowman dusted flakes from
Little Rabbit's fur and lifted
him onto his shoulders.

"I'll take you home," he said.
"Hold on tight!"

They slid down the hill. . .

WHOOOOOOOOOSH!

And landed in a snowy heap
by a frozen stream. WHUMPH!

"Here we go!" Snowman laughed as he held Little Rabbit's paw.

The world whisked by in a shimmer of silver frost. It felt as if they were flying.

"I'm coming home, Daddy!" Little Rabbit called.

WHEEEEEEEEEEE!

Suddenly, Snowman skidded to a halt at the
bottom of a hill.

"We'll have to walk now," he said, as he
swung Little Rabbit into his soft arms.

"Are we there yet?" yawned Little Rabbit.

"Not far now," said Snowman.

Meanwhile, Daddy Rabbit was hurrying through the whirling snow. He was very worried and he shivered in the icy wind.

"Little Rabbit!" he called. "Little Rabbit! Where are you?"

"Daddy!" cried Little Rabbit when
he heard his call. He leaped from
Snowman's arms and bounded up
the garden.

Daddy Rabbit swept him up
and hugged him tight, forgetting
all about the berries.
   "Thank goodness you're safe!"
he said. "I was so worried about
you, all alone."

"I wasn't alone," said Little Rabbit. "Snowman
took care of me."

"Oh, did he now?" Daddy chuckled.

Snowman stood quietly in the winter darkness.
Little Rabbit smiled at him. And he saw Snowman
was smiling, too.